Usborne
That's not my...
Jungle
Activity book

Find me on every double page.

Matthew Oldham

Illustrated by Rachel Wells

Designed by Josephine Thompson,
Eleanor Stevenson & Hannah Ahmed

Based on the Usborne touchy-feely That's not my... series.

That's my elephant

Draw more leaves for your elephant to eat.

Where are you, little white mouse?

Yum, yum...

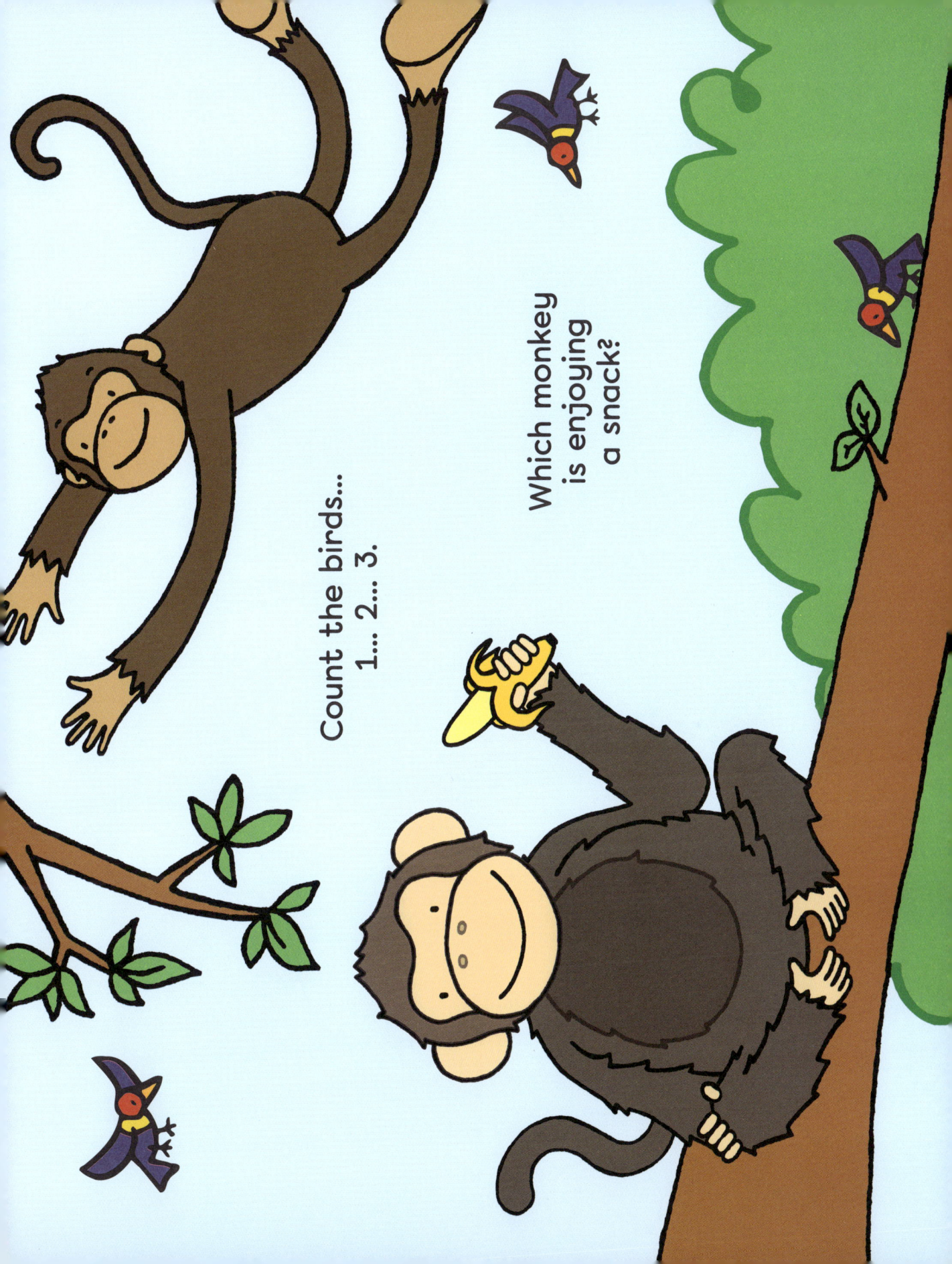

That's my leopard

Please add more spots to my coat.

Look for the little white mouse.

Spot the differences between the pictures above. There are FOUR to find.

That's my butterfly

Fill in your butterfly.

Little white mouse, where are you?

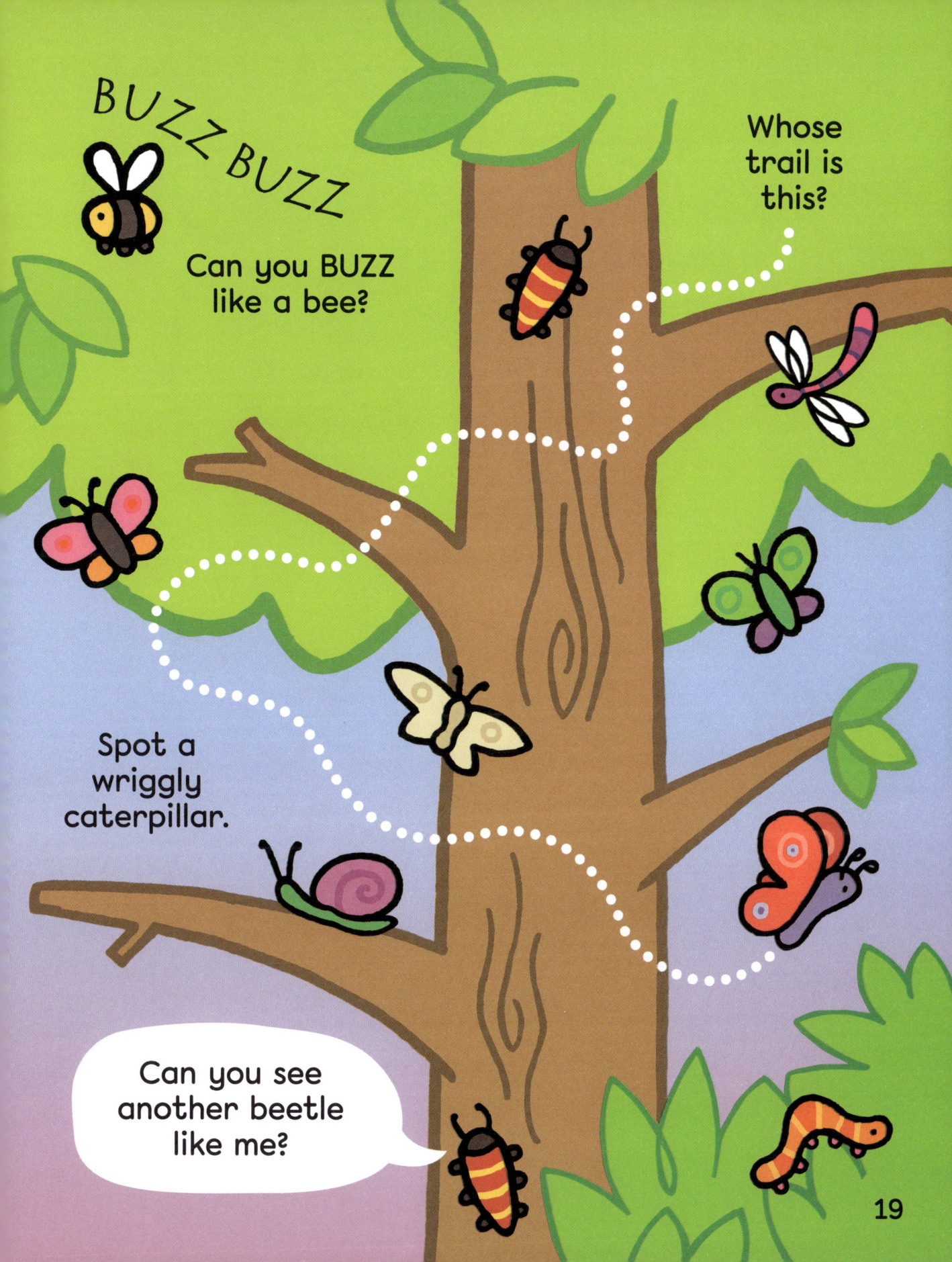

That's my gorilla

Fill in your gorilla's eyebrows.
Draw a smile, too.

Can you hoot
like a gorilla?

Ooh-ooh-ooh

Find the
little white
mouse.

Spot the differences between these scenes.
There are FOUR to find.

21

That's my jungle

Where is the little white mouse?

Can you spot the differences between these pictures? There are FIVE to find.

Who does NOT belong in the jungle?

Jungle at night

Some jungle creatures only come out at night.

Which bat is upside down?

Find FIVE fireflies...
1... 2... 3... 4... 5.

Please fill in my body.

Look for the little white mouse.